Penguin

by Liza Charlesworth

ISBN: 978-1-338-78277-6
Illustrated by Roger Simó
Copyright © 2021 by Liza Charlesworth. All rights reserved.
Published by Scholastic Inc., 557 Broadway, New York, NY 10012

10 9 8 7 6 5 4 3 2 1   68   21 22 23 24 25 26 27/0

Printed in Jiaxing, China. First printing, June 2021.

We are two penguin pals.
We love to hop and hop!

2

We are two penguin pals.
We love to walk and walk!

We are two penguin pals.
We love to talk and talk!

We are two penguin pals.
We love to slide and slide!

We are two penguin pals.
We love to dive and dive!

We are two penguin pals.
We love to swim and swim!

We are two penguin pals.
We love to ride and ride!